the Lipstick

Laura Dockrill

illustrated by
Maria Karipidou

WALKER BOOKS
AND SUBSIDIARIES
LONDON • BOSTON • SYDNEY • AUCKLAND

For Jet ~ L.D.   For Miro ~ M.K.

First published 2021 by Walker Books Ltd, 87 Vauxhall Walk, London SE11 5HJ • Text © 2021 Laura Dockrill • Illustrations © 2021 Maria Karipidou • The right of Laura Dockrill and Maria Karipidou to be identified as author and illustrator respectively of this work has been asserted by them in accordance with the Copyright, Designs and Patents Act 1988 • This book has been typeset in Neutraface Display • Printed in China • All rights reserved. No part of this book may be reproduced, transmitted or stored in an information retrieval system in any form or by any means, graphic, electronic or mechanical, including photocopying, taping and recording, without prior written permission from the publisher. British Library Cataloguing in Publication Data: a catalogue record for this book is available from the British Library • ISBN 978-1-4063-8955-5 • www.walker.co.uk • 10 9 8 7 6 5 4 3 2 1

They say they ALWAYS know you're up
to something when the house goes quiet...

And today the house was very, very quiet.

Oooooh look!
Mum’s posh lipstick.

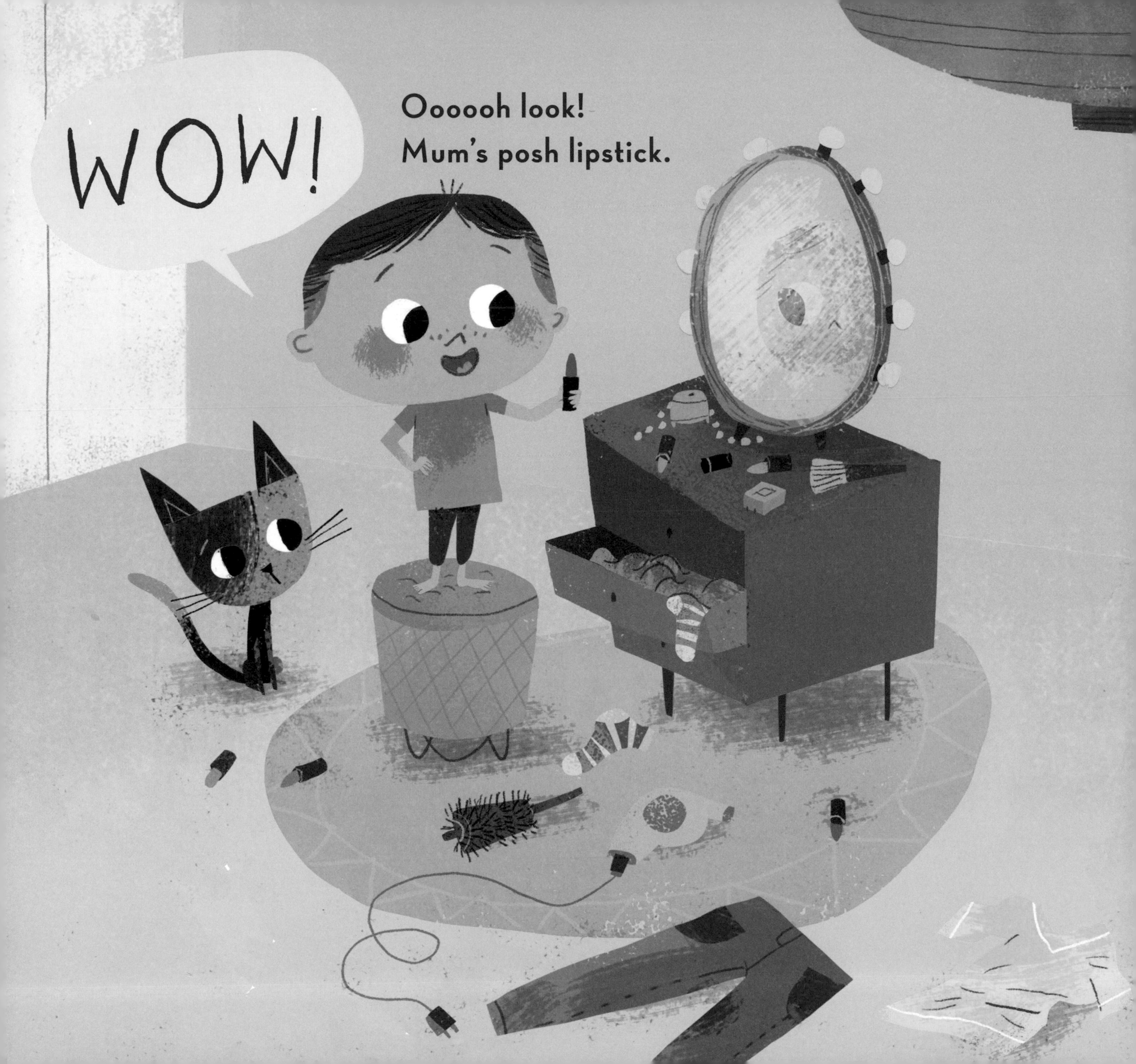

Looking in the mirror, I pressed the lipstick ever so softly against my lips like how exactly Mum does, trying to be so careful to keep inside the lines...

Only some bits did go OUTSIDE the lines.

I did a kiss in the mirror.

MWAH!

I did look LOVELY,
if I do say so myself.

I took the lipstick for a little walk.

Doodling and oodling and noodling and poodling ... and whatever else rhymes with doodling.

I even pressed down hard like how you're not meant to.

I simply drew any old picture that came
into my head, to be honest.
I wanted to write my name but didn't,
because this is a SECRET
but I can't actually spell right now
at this point in my life.

I drew
a hedgehog,

a shoe,

a frilly dress,

a corn on a cob,

a boxing glove...

WHATEVER!
This was so simply GREAT.
This was like ... I don't know ...
MAYBE even ...

the best day
of my actual LIFE.

I let the lipstick be in charge.

It wanted me to go downstairs.
I think.

It's not ME, guys,
it's the lipstick.
It has a mind of its own!

It prettied up the shiny bathroom tiles ... and our fluffy, scruffy cat, Martin.

(Oh, Lipstick, that's terribly NAUGHTY!)

It scribbled
on the fridge ...

the apples ...

and the photos of us.

(A quick cookie break.)

Just making the whole house
ABSOLUTELY gorgeous
and colourful.

I ran into Bug's room (which SHHH by the way I'm NEVER allowed to be in). I just had to go wherever the lipstick wanted me to go, didn't I?

And besides anyway my sister likes ALL colours.
And besides how could anybody
NOT like the lipstick?

Then I heard FOOTSTEPS...
I threw the lipstick under the sofa really quickly
and tried to look clean.

But it was no good.
The lipstick had most
certainly BETRAYED me –
which means letting somebody down.

The lipstick had ruined my actual life.
I knew I couldn't trust that PESKY thing.

IT WAS THE LIPSTICK!

All I was doing was making the whole house **ABSOLUTELY** gorgeous and colourful.

SORRY...

I even said. But SORRY didn't cut it.

And the lipstick didn't say sorry once.
It just sat there looking all pleased with itself.

We had to clean
down the STAIRS,

Bug's ANNOYING ROOM,

the BATHROOM

and all along the WALLS.

But there was ONE PLACE
I was NOT going to clean the lipstick off.

Because that is where lipstick belongs.
And I look really GREAT.